SCOOBY DOO 2

MONSTERS UNLEASHED

Adapted by Jesse
Leon McCann

WB WORLDWIDE PUBLISHING

Scholastic Inc.
New York   Toronto   London   Auckland   Sydney
Mexico City   New Delhi   Hong Kong   Buenos Aires

ISBN 0-439-57862-0

Designed by Louise Bova

12 11 10 9 8 7 6 5 4 3 2 1   4 5 6 7 8 9/0
Printed in the U.S.A.
First printing, March 2004

Fred, Daphne, Velma, Shaggy, and Scooby-Doo were going to a big party at the Coolsonian Criminology Museum. The museum was holding a special exhibit of all the creatures and villains the gang had ever unmasked. The party was a formal affair, so everyone was dressed up — even Scooby, Shaggy, and Velma.

Shaggy with Patrick,
the museum's curator

Patrick, the museum's curator, greeted them when they arrived at the museum. So did a bunch of their screaming fans!

"May I have a word with Coolsville's hottest detectives?" asked Heather, a local TV reporter.

Heather's cameraman, Ned, was videotaping the event.

"Absolutely," answered Fred.

"Well, there you go, there's your word," Daphne said to Heather as she pulled Fred away. "Come on, we're late."

It seemed to Fred that Daphne didn't like Heather. Or maybe she was just jealous.

Inside the museum, costumes of the many scary villains that Mystery, Inc. had unmasked in the past were on display.

"We're proud to donate these costumes to the museum," Fred told the crowd. "There are over two hundred costumes in these glass cases."

Just then, there was a loud *CRASH!* The Pterodactyl Ghost costume had come to life and broken out of its glass case!

A masked figure appeared out of nowhere. "Come, my pet, and bring my prizes!" the figure cackled.

The pterodactyl grabbed two costumes and flew away, carrying the masked figure away on its back.

The Mystery, Inc. kids tried to stop the monsters, but they got away!

The next day, Heather reported what had happened at the museum. But she made it sound like it was the gang's fault that the masked figure got away with the costumes. In fact, Heather said that Shaggy and Scooby were bumbling idiots!

"Ruh-roh," Scooby said sadly. He and Shaggy felt like pretty lousy detectives.

Scooby and Shaggy were so ashamed. It was their fault all the monsters had escaped. They decided they needed to become better detectives, like their friends Fred, Velma, and Daphne.

"Like, to be better detectives, we decided to dress like better detectives," Shaggy told his friends.

"Okay, but don't stretch out my sweater," Velma warned him. She was analyzing a pterodactyl scale that she had found at the museum. "Jinkies! My tests say the pterodactyl was real, not a costume!"

Shaggy, dressed like Fred

"But who would be able to create a real Pterodactyl Ghost?" asked Velma.

"The original Pterodactyl Ghost we once captured, Dr. Jonathan Jacobo!" Daphne replied. "I bet he's behind it."

"I don't think so," Fred said. "Jacobo was lost at sea while attempting to escape from an island prison."

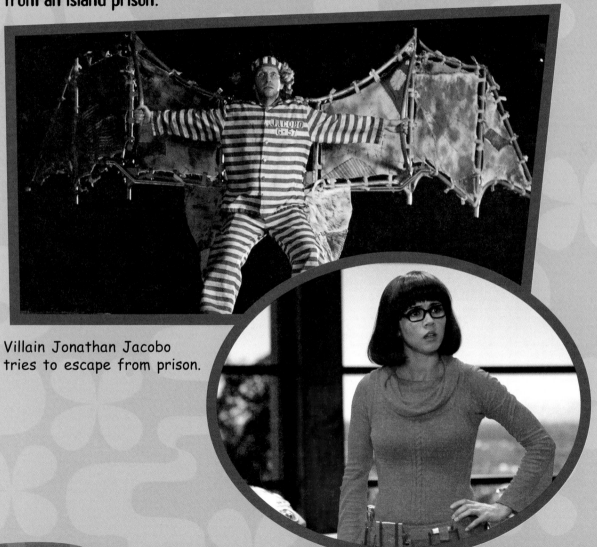

Villain Jonathan Jacobo tries to escape from prison.

"What about this?" Daphne said. "Dr. Jacobo's cellmate, Jeremiah Wickles, was released from prison two months ago."

"He was the Black Knight Ghost, one of the costumes that was stolen from the museum!" exclaimed Fred. "I think we need to pay Old Man Wickles a visit!"

"Here we are, 505 Troll Court, Jeremiah Wickles' mansion," Velma said.

"Oh, man, another creepy crib!" Shaggy complained. "Like, why don't we ever get to investigate a hamburger stand or something?"

"Reah, ramburgers!" Scooby nodded and licked his lips hungrily.

When Fred pushed the doorbell, a voice boomed through a speaker, "LEAVE NOW OR PAY THE PRICE! YOU HAVE BEEN WARNED!"

"Like, don't do it, Fred!" Shaggy cried. "We have been warned!"

"What could possibly happen by pushing a doorbell?" Fred asked, pushing it again. All of a sudden, a trapdoor opened beneath the gang, and they tumbled into darkness!

The gang was trapped inside a cage shaped like a ball in Old Man Wickles' basement. But Daphne managed to figure out a way to escape. Then the gang split up to look for clues. Before long, the kids had discovered some very important information — like a musty old book called *How to Make Monsters*, and glowing footprints on the floor!

But the gang didn't have time to find out what these clues meant. Without warning, the Black Knight Ghost appeared in front of Scooby and Shaggy. The two buddies ran for their lives! Fortunately, they soon found Fred, Daphne, and Velma — and Velma managed to outsmart the Black Knight Ghost. It was time to get out of Old Man Wickles' mansion before any new monsters appeared!

Fred and the girls returned to the museum to look for more clues. And they couldn't believe what they saw — it was in shambles!

"There's been another robbery!" cried Patrick. "*All* the costumes have been stolen . . . by monsters!"

To make matters worse, Heather and her news crew arrived and blamed everything on Mystery, Inc.

At the same time, Shaggy and Scooby were following a clue that they had discovered in Old Man Wickles' mansion. It led them to a nightclub, the Faux Ghost, where villains liked to hang out. They were all crooks that Mystery, Inc. had caught and unmasked in the past.

Scooby and Shaggy figured that they'd be in big trouble if the bad guys found out who they were, so they pretended to be criminals, too. Shaggy even managed to talk to Old Man Wickles. But unfortunately, Scooby attracted a lot of attention.

It didn't take long for the criminals to recognize Scooby and Shaggy.

"That's Scooby-Doo, the meddling mutt who helped throw us in jail!" sneered one crook. "And that's his beatnik best pal, Shaggy Rogers!"

"Zoinks!" Shaggy gulped as he and Scooby ran from the crooked bullies. "Like, gangway!"

They leaped over the bar, slid down a laundry chute, and left the criminals far behind!

Outside, Scooby and Shaggy saw someone leaving the nightclub. It was Old Man Wickles! They decided to follow him.

"Hey, Scoob. Like, look! Old Man Wickles led us right into The Old Tyme Mining Town. Zoinks! It's, like, a spooky ghost town!" Shaggy said.

"Rhost rown?" Scooby gasped.

They followed Old Man Wickles to a deserted old building. Now he was having a secret meeting with some mysterious men.

Shaggy and Scooby tried to sneak closer, but something stopped them. A big freaky, one-eyed monster!

Meanwhile, Velma had analyzed a sample of the glowing footprints from the mansion. She discovered that they glowed because of a mineral called randamonium, found only in The Old Tyme Mining Town.

As Velma, Fred, and Daphne sneaked into the town, they saw Old Man Wickles meeting with some mysterious men. Fred was sure that they would catch the men planning a crime!

"A-ha!" Fred shouted. "Old Man Wickles, we've caught you red-handed in your foul, monster-making scheme with your ugly, evil henchmen!"

But Fred was wrong. Old Man Wickles was meeting with businessmen, hoping that they would invest money and turn the deserted old town into an amusement park.

Meanwhile, Scooby and Shaggy were still running from the freaky monster. They escaped underground, where they discovered a hidden lab. Unfortunately, they accidentally spilled some strange scientific potions all over themselves. Big mistake! They were instantly transformed into monsters! Shaggy turned into a muscleman! Scooby grew a huge brain! But luckily, Scooby was so smart that he was able to mix a potion that turned them back to normal.

Fred, Daphne, and Velma finally caught up with Scooby and Shaggy, who were staring through a huge hole in the wall Shaggy had made while under the effects of Scooby's concoction.

"This must be where the evil masked figure turns the costumes into real monsters," Daphne said.

Fred was amazed. "They're all here! Every costume from every villain we've unmasked!"

"Like, it's pretty dark," Shaggy commented. "Maybe we can find a light switch."

Scooby and Shaggy found a big switch and flipped it on. Instantly, a machine lit up and started humming. The two buddies were pretty pleased with themselves . . . until they realized that they had activated the monster-making machine! Costumes were turning into real monsters all around them!

"Disconnect the control panel, Shaggy!" Velma yelled. "That will stop the machine from making more creatures!"

Fred grabbed the control panel, and they fled from the monsters as fast as they could.

The evil masked figure appeared. "Stop them!" he commanded the monsters. "Retrieve my control panel!"

It looked as if the creepy creatures would capture the gang as they rode the elevator up. The Mystery, Inc. kids barely managed to escape.

Scooby and Shaggy were sad. Some detectives they were! Thanks to them, a hundred monsters were on the loose.

The gang had to hide out in their old high school clubhouse. But Velma had a plan. She used a homemade computer to reprogram the control panel.

"Once we reconnect this to the monster-making machine and flip the switch on, all the monsters will be destroyed," Velma explained.

Getting the control panel back to the masked villain's lair wasn't easy! The gang was attacked by all sorts of monsters, including the Black Knight Ghost.

"Zoinks!" cried Shaggy. "This is tied for the most terrifying day of my life!"

"Tied with what?" Velma asked.

"With, like, every *other* day of my life!" Shaggy answered.

The Mystery Machine zoomed wildly through the streets of Coolsville. Fred made some crazy turns, causing the Pterodactyl Ghost to fly right into a billboard.

There was also a zombie driving an eighteen-wheeler truck. It took a lot of fancy driving on Fred's part to escape him. Finally, the gang was heading out of town, leaving the monsters in the dust.

"*Roo-hoo!*" Scooby cheered. Then he laughed. "*Ree-hee-hee-hee!*"

When the gang got to the lab, it seemed deserted — until they were suddenly surrounded by dozens of snarling, cackling monsters!

"Go long, Shaggy!" Velma yelled. "Only you and Scooby can save us now!"

"But . . . " Shaggy began. He was afraid of letting the gang down again.

Velma gazed at him and Scooby. "Shaggy, you and Scooby have been heroes all along. You just didn't know it. You can do this!"

She tossed him the control panel. Shaggy caught the control panel and passed it to Scooby, who snapped it in place.

"Scooby. Dooby. Doo," he declared triumphantly.

"NOOOO!" cried the masked villain as his monsters melted into harmless goo.

Velma looked at Daphne. "If our hunch is correct, the person behind all this is . . ."

". . . Heather, the TV reporter!" Daphne shouted. "With help from Ned, her cameraman."

"But why did she do it?" asked one of the newsmen.

Velma smiled. "Because Heather is actually Dr. Jacobo, who wanted revenge against us!"

"You always were a troublemaker, Jacobo!" growled Old Man Wickles.

Scooby and Shaggy grinned at each other. "Another mystery solved!" Shaggy cried. It was Fred's line, but this time Shaggy knew that he and Scooby were the real heroes. And they'd saved the day just by being themselves. "Like, I guess we're pretty swell detectives after all, right, Scoob?"

"*Rooby-dooby-doo!*" cheered Scooby-Doo.